對 流

CONVECTION

夏菁中英對照詩集
A Chinese-English Bilingual Anthology

By Hsia Ching

By Hsia Ching

前　言

　　從一九五〇年代末起，我就開始翻譯若干英美詩人的詩，全憑興趣，並無系統。最引以為榮的是，所譯美國詩人佛勞斯特（Robert Frost）的詩，有六首被納入《美國詩選》（一九六一，今日世界社出版），和梁實秋、張愛玲、余光中等等的譯作同列。其後，我因公務繁忙、出國深造、繼而到聯合國工作，少再迻譯。其中有好多年，連詩也少寫，不要說翻譯了。

　　迄至上世紀末，我從聯合國、科羅拉多州立大學、以及國際顧問工作退休以後，又漸漸對譯詩恢復興趣。先是，在二〇〇四年，將友人余光中、馬寬、陶忘機（John J.S. Balcom）等歷年來譯我的詩，交香港銀河出版社出版。集名《夏菁短詩選》。近年來，因參加了在美唯一的中、英雙語網路詩刊〈詩天空〉（Poetrysky），就開始認真地英譯自己的詩。

　　我覺得譯自己的詩，至少有兩個好處。第一，將兩種文字對比，常常使我認知中文在時態和主詞上的曖昧，從而對我中文詩的創作，有所警惕。第二是譯自己的詩，享有一種自由度，可以在不損原意的前提下，遣句選字，享有彈性。我喜用淺顯的語言來寫詩，因此，翻譯起來，並不過份困難；至於是否典雅，只能由讀者去判斷。

　　這本集子分成三輯。第一輯是英譯我自己的中文詩,共三十首。第二輯是我中譯英美詩人的作品,計二十三首。最後一輯是友人英譯我的詩,包括以前未能納入《夏菁短詩選》的以及新譯者,共二十首。這一輯的詩大多已在中華民國筆會的季刊上刊載過。

　　人說:詩是不能翻譯的。我相信譯者只要盡力而為,使譯文盡量接近原作即可。我覺得,中、英詩對照排列,猶如大氣的對流(一個是外來、一個是當地),這本詩集是否會激起詩天空的一點火花和回響,將拭目以待。

　　馬嬴、Dona Stein、黃用、〈詩天空〉主編韓怡丹(綠音)、及編輯 K.D. Anderson 諸位潤飾或編輯我的英譯,感激不盡。余光中、馬嬴、陶忘機、王季文等位迻譯我的中文詩,以及〈筆會〉、〈詩天空〉等刊出這些詩;盛杭英的協校此書,在茲一併致謝。

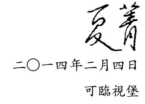

二〇一四年二月四日

可臨視堡

Preface

I started translating some English and American poems into Chinese from the late 1950's, purely for personal interest. I felt most honored when my translations of six Robert Frost poems were published in the *Anthology of American Poetry* (World Today, Hong Kong, 1961) alongside with several famous writers including Professor Liang Shih-chiu, Yu Kwang-chung, and Eileen Chang. However, throughout the following two decades, because of my professional duty, studying in the United States, and working at FAO of the United Nations, I gradually produced less poems, let alone translations.

Towards the end of last Century, when I retired from UN, from teaching at Colorado State University and international consulting work, I revived my interest in translations. First, I collected English translations of my poems by Professor Yu Kwang-chung, Wei Ma, John J.S. Balcom and others, and published them in *Selected Poems of Hsia Ching* (The Milkway Published Co., Hong Kong, 2004). Recently, I joined the Poetrysky Journal, a Chinese-English poetry website magazine, and started seriously to translate my own poems into English.

I discovered some advantages in translating my own poems. First, a close comparison between two languages often detects the structural ambiguities of the Chinese (i.e. the lack of tenses and subjects). This makes me more aware of my own writing of Chinese poems. Secondly, translating own poems could enjoy the flexibility and freedom of word choice as long as the original meaning is not impaired. I often use simple and common language in my Chinese poems. Therefore, less difficulties are encountered when translating them into English. Whether they are elegant or not are for the readers to judge.

This anthology contains three parts. The first part includes thirty of my poems which are translated into English by myself. The second part contains twenty three English poems which I translated into Chinese. The last part consists of twenty of my poems translated by my friends into English. These translations are not included in my previous publication and the majority of them have been published in the *Quarterly Journal of Contemporary Chinese Literature* by the Taipei Chinese Center, International PEN.

People say poetry cannot be translated. But I believe that what a translator can do is to do his or her best to make the translation as close to the original work as possible. I also feel that bilingual poems presented on opposite pages resemble the air convection of the atmosphere (one foreign and one native). Whether this volume will eventually cause some sparks and echoes in the poetry sky remains to be seen.

I am deeply indebted to Messrs Wei Ma, Dona Stein, Charles Huang, and Poetrysky Journal's Yidan Han and Kyle D. Anderson for their editing of my English translations. Also, I sincerely thank Messrs. Yu Kwang-chung, Wei Ma, John J.S. Balcom, C.W. Wang, for their translations of my poems into English. Thanks are also due to The Taipei Chinese PEN and Poetrysky Journal for publishing these poems and, finally, to Julietta Sheng, my granddaughter, for her assisting in editing and proof reading of this volume.

Hsia Ching

February 4, 2014

Fort Collins, Colorado

目　錄

CONTENTS

第二輯：中譯
—— 夏菁譯英美詩人的詩

Part Two：Chinese Translations

Author's Translations of English poems into Chinese

Robert Frost   103

D.H. Lawrence   123

第三輯：友譯
——友人英譯夏菁的詩

Part Three: Friends' Translations

Friends' Translations of Hsia Ching's Poems into English

C.W. Wang   161

John J.S. Balcom   179

對流
CONVECTION

第一輯：英譯
——夏菁譯自已的詩

Part One: English Translations
Author's translations of his own poems into English

紫丁香盛開　Lilac is in Full Bloom.

獨　行

在四顧茫茫的雪地
一個人踽踽獨行
沒有風，也無鳥啼
唯有雪的寧靜

我闖入一片林裡
只聽到自己的跫音
車聲已遠在天際
我有顆不競的心

回頭所能看見
一徑鴻爪般的腳印
這些能否留到明天？
誰也不能肯定

也沒有什麼理由
踏上這一條僻徑
現在，已快到盡頭
無悔，靠一點自信

Walking Alone

Walking in a vast, snowy field
I was alone and moving slow
No wind, not even a crying bird
But, the silence of snow

Then I intruded into a piece of woods
Only my footsteps echoed behind
Traffic noises were left over the horizon
What I kept was my peace of mind

Looking backward all I could see
Was a trail of footprints left by me
Whether they could last till tomorrow?
Surely no one could foresee

Nor was there any good reason, why
I should take this secluded course
Now, I have almost reached its end
No regret, I hold out my confidence

車過冰湖

車道轉彎處忽然瞥見
白茫茫的一隻盲眼
看起來似曾相識，只是
想不起他的名字

哦！去夏我曾到過那裡
綠汪汪、眼波依依
現在卻矇上白內障一層
毛玻璃透不出真情

這種計較，也許錯在我自己
人老去，總愛和從前相比
湖還是湖，哪有什麼改變？
到現在，我也有很多盲點

不久，春風會在一夜之間
將湖水的心結一一化解
我妒嫉他享有這種輪迴
心中又不禁感到慚愧

Driving by a Frozen Lake

Driving around a corner suddenly I see
A whitish blind eye passing me
I seemed to have known it for a long time
But could not recall its name

Oh, I was actually there last summer
A greenish eye filled with active motion
Now, it is covered with cataract
Frosted glass that reveals no emotion

This kind of sentiment is probably my fault
Growing old one tends to compare things with the past
A lake is still a lake, what changes can it make?
By now, I myself have also many blind spots

Soon the spring breeze will melt away overnight
All the harden parts from the lake's heart
I was jealous of its capacity to restart a life cycle
Immediately, I am ashamed of such a thought

消　息

冬天常常駛過一個農莊
馬、冷落的鉛絲網
樹、乾涸的河床

今早，我忽然覺得
有一些異樣
嫩柳在絲絲飄忽
牡馬在頻頻昂仰

馬、樹和我之間
互傳著什麼消息？
或僅僅是為了一片
乍暖的空氣

A Message

I often drove by a farm in winter
Horses, barbwire fences of cold
Trees, and a dried stream bed

I suddenly felt this morning
Something was unusual
Fresh willow branches were swinging
And stallions were restless and leaping

Amongst horses, trees, and I
What message are we trying to imply?
Or is it just, just owing to
Some warmer air goes through

春之來

春之來
自陣陣迎面的風中
柔柔像紗帕的戲弄

春之來
從停停歇歇的雨裡
絲絲將新綠梳洗

春之來
在千呼萬喚的中途
鬱金香終於出土

在冰雪初融的溪裡
春之來
汩汩似我的脈息

在眼前、耳際和唇邊
春之來
若詩的不可避免

Spring is Arriving

Spring is arriving

In the intermittent breeze blowing to my face

Soft and playful, like handkerchief's brushing

Spring is arriving

In the rains that come and go

Washing and combing gently the newly green

Spring is arriving

Amid hundreds of bird calls

The tulips that are finally sprouting

In the creeks with newly melting ice

Spring is arriving

Rhythmically like the beating of my pulse

Through my eyes, ears and lips

Spring is arriving

As inevitable as poems' spontaneous

春 雪

春雪夾帶著和靄的氣氛
灑落著片片的柔情
假如對嚴冬你感到厭棄
現在會掀起再生的歡喜

在這一年開始的時光
總會有一種希冀和渴望
不管今年會帶給我們
什麼樣的喧鬧或繽紛

此刻，世界是如此靜謐
遠遠只聽到微風的呼吸
可是，它短得像一幕啞劇
受不了太陽的逼視和妒嫉

看著一片片落地即融的雪花
今生今世有什麼可以真正留下？

Spring Snow

Spring snow brings a warm atmosphere
By scattering pieces of tender flakes
If you were tired with the severe winter
You can now rejoice with renewed awareness

At the year's very beginning
There is always certain longing and yearning
No matter what the new year can finally bring
Pure noises or a colorful ending

At this moment, however, the world is tranquil so
You can hear the breeze faintly breathing afar
But the scene was as brief as a pantomime show
Owing to sun's jealousy and sternly stare

Looking at flakes quick-melting on the ground
I wonder what my life could really leave behind?

紫丁香盛開

紫丁香在園中盛開
一年一度的企盼
那暗香飄走我的構思
撩人的還有她的色彩

一簇簇細緻的十字星
紫紅色平添浪漫的氣氛
僅僅也只有這麼幾天
色褪了還要等到明年

春天為何要向人挑戰
這麼短暫，卻這麼姣好
我不怕自己將垂垂老去
只惋惜看花的日子更少

The Lilac is in Full Bloom

The lilac in my garden is in full bloom
An once a year event for expectation
Her aroma is luring away my thoughts
And her color is an enchanting flirtation

The flowers have many clusters of fine crosses
The purple hues enhance the romantic atmosphere
Yet, all of these will last only a day or two
Once fading, it won't be back for another year

Spring is so splendid, yet it is so short
Why should it challenge us all
I am not afraid of getting older and older
Regret only my lesser days to watch flower

風信子

風信子，風信子
提起你的名字
我就有不斷的遐思
當春風吹開三月的寒襟
你已守信地玉立亭亭
你的光彩會媲美
海倫的髮絲
你再生的傳說
是希臘最早的故事

風信子，風信子
你對我卻有
另一種的暗示
說不出、只能會意
如早春的迷惘
夢後的癡疑
往者已矣，逝者已矣
如果一定要追問
我最多奉告如次：

Hyacinth

Hyacinth, Hyacinth

Every time your name is mentioned

I could not hold back my imagination

When the spring breeze opens March's cold collar

You are already there, slim and graceful

Your brilliant color has been compared

Favorably with Helen's hair

And your legend of rebirth

Is Greek's earliest tale

Hyacinth, Hyacinth

You actually hold

A different kind of hint to me

It cannot be said, but only to be felt

Like the daze of the spring

Like a dream over hanging

Let bygones be bygones; what's passed is passed

If anyone insists to ask

My answer is mostly like this:

向空中默誦一個名字
再想想以前那段
揮不去影子
茶飯不思的日子

Silently utter a name towards the sky

Then think about those old days

When you could not wave off the image

When you went without food all day

夏末的感覺

夏末有一種異樣的陽光
像人到中年漸收起青芒
興高采烈的日子已屬過去
心情若學童般回到課堂

遠山已展示一種黛色
黃葉像獨木舟漂在草上
那些縱情或懶散的往事
會在日記中漸漸淡忘

九月將有隻多淚的眼睛
不像盛夏那樣地開朗
過掉孳長及飽滿的一季
瘦了的秋等我們去欣賞

Feelings at the End of Summer

At the end of Summer the sun changes its light
As a mid-aged man becoming less sharp and bright
Gone are all the exciting days of season past
Now, feelings are like the children back to school at last

The distant hills present a touch of darkish green
Some yellow leaves fall on the lawn like canoes drifting
Memories of either indulgence or of lazy days
Will be slowly fading away from our diaries

Yet, September will have its wet and teary eyes
Unlike the mid-summer days bright and clear
After a season of overgrowth and saturation
The newly slimmed Autumn is awaiting our appreciation

窗前的白楊

窗前有一棵白楊樹
在秋風裡瑟瑟作聲
不知道他在絮絮些什麼
我常常是聽而不聞

他的葉片是小小的心臟
樹身上有一隻隻眼睛
也許他看到我在燈下凝思
我卻不能領會他的關心

他似乎在說：秋天太短
金色的葉片已快掉盡
或許他在暗中羨慕著我
降雪時有一個屋頂

我倒是十分妒嫉他
葉子掉盡還可以重生
春往秋來，我會老去
有一天見不到我的蹤影

An Aspen at My Window

At my window there is an aspen tree
In the autumn wind he is rustling
I do not know what his whispering may be
Often, I heard him without listening

His leaves are hearts of miniature size
And his trunk grows many eyes
He may have seen me pondering under a lantern
But I have never sensed his concern

He seems to say: Autumn is too brief
Almost all my golden leaves are dead
Outside in the dark, he might envy me
When snow starts I have a roof over my head

In fact, I am quite jealous of him
Leaves can die and grow again for sure
But, year after year, I will only grow older
Until one day he won't see me anymore

他原自雪山皚皚的溪邊
我遷自亞熱帶的雨林
兩棵移植的樹不期而遇
一個怕長年輪、一個無根

註：白楊（Aspen）栽在海拔不高之處，壽命不長。

In a snowy mountain creek he originated
From a sub-tropical rain forest I migrated
Two transplanted trees meet here by chance
He worries about rings, and I, about my roots

Note: Aspens cannot survive long at lower elevation.

夜望星空

夜望星空
浩瀚無窮
但願他們都屬
輪迴的星宿

不論在世時他們
曾經辛苦一生
或僅驚鴻一瞥
現在他們都以
脈脈的星眸
觀照前塵
滄海一粟般地
守望著我們

在這星移斗轉之間
我要找出一張臉龐
和它星圖上的坐標
將來好飛去探訪

Watching the Starlit Night

Watching the starlit night
I find no boundary in sight
I hope all of its stars
Belong to Samsara

Their lives on earth, whether was long
And hard, or simply a flick of a moment
Filled with excitement
They are now all watching the earth
With tender glistening eyes
And recalling their old memories
Meanwhile, they painstakingly watch
And guide us, through the boundless universe

Among these ever-moving stars
I want to find a familiar face
With her coordinates at the star chart
To facilitate my eternal visit in the space

滿滿的一袋風

我有久藏的
口袋一只
現在裝著空空
我早年的相思
寂寞的楓紅
和我的詩意
還沒有一個字

神話、不是
哲學、不是
刻骨的往事、是
但早已經消逝
現在剩下的只是
滿滿的一袋風
和白楊的瑟瑟

A Pocket of Wind

I have a pocket

That is decades old

It now holds an empty space

Of my love memory

With maples' melancholy

And my poetic thoughts

Yet without a word

A myth, no

A philosophy, no

A heart-wrenching past, yes

That has faded fast

What's left now is nothing

But a pocket of wind

And aspen's rustling

沒有風的日子

沒有風的日子
雲，不再飄逸
鳥聲不颺
我屋簷下的
風鈴，不叮叮作響

口哨也頻吹不起
遐思不再
信差不來
昨日的激情已矣
只好將風箏掛起

沒有風的日子
也沒有念詩

一切似墜入夢底
只待一聲呼喚
只等一絲信息

The Day There is no Wind

The day there is no wind
No more are flying clouds
Neither birds sing aloud
My wind chimes under the eaves
Stopped their tinkling sound

No more are my whistling
No more are my fancy thinking
And no more is a postman coming
The excitement of yesterday died
I had better hang-up my kite

The day there is no wind
Neither is any poem read

All seem to fall to the bottom of a dream
Waiting only for a distant call
Waiting only for a faint message

六千年的擁抱
——一對義大利發掘的骸骨

時間在他們的擁抱裡
已消失了意義
六千年，只是昨天
當初是這般睡姿
現在還是

白骨相擁
還有什麼、在這個世間
更使人感動？
他們擁抱在傳說以前
歷史之前，也許
那時還沒有文字
沒有適當的語言

就是這樣一個擁姿
使人黯然拭淚
使人低頭沉思
他們的肢體語言
勝過、將愛說上一千遍

Eternal Embrace
A pair of skeletons discovered at Southern Italy

Since they embraced together
Time has lost its meaning
Six thousand years seem like yesterday
They poised in that same position then
And still do so this day

Skeletons in an eternal embrace
Is there anything in the world
More touching than this?
They embraced before we had any legends
Before history, or perhaps
Before any meaningful written signs
Let alone a descriptive language

This very embrace
Makes us sorrowfully shed tears
And sink into our deep reflection
Their body language says a lot more
Than uttering " Love" for a thousand times

一首無言的傑作
不需要任何解說
在這種至死不渝之前
莎士比亞變得饒舌
我的更加靦腆

A masterpiece of wordless devotion

Does not need any interpretation

In front of this scene of eternal love

Shakespeare would become loquacious

And my work, bashfully worthless

後院採李子

枝條已經壓到了地面
一種成熟的長髮披肩
纍纍地透出紅潤的光彩
走過的都想伸手一採

她說：「這樹長在我們的籬內
果子卻也向鄰居低垂」
我暗想：大自然豈會分界限？
彼此分享是睦鄰的起點

她帶上手套，伸手要採
我說：「手套將造成一層隔膜
會失卻人和大自然的接觸
那種柔柔、溫溫地一握
一季的陽光和雨水才將之充足」

採了又採，禁不住地貪婪
將高高的枝條用力地拉下來
拉到像一隻隻弓的張開

Picking Plums in Backyard

Many branches bent toward the ground
A kind of matured long hair we found
Bountiful are the red fruits shinning
Anyone who passes would tempt a picking

She murmured: "The tree grows at our site
Yet many fruits hang over to neighbor's side"
I mused: Does Nature observe boundary of land?
Sharing is probably the base of making friend

She put on gloves and started picking
I said: "Gloves create a layer of separation
Of human and Nature's intimate touching
A grasp of soft and warm feeling
Is the result of season's sunlight and watering"

Plums after plums, we couldn't stop picking
Greed driven, we pulled down the higher branches
And bent them like fully drawn bows

當她說：「也要給知更鳥留一點」
剎那間、樹枝就反彈上青天

一隻黃蜂在頭頂迴繞
像是給我們一種警告
我答稱：「這樣也好，不用梯子
留一些給松鼠、留一些給孩子——
不要任意將他們的世界毀掉！
也讓這棵樹漸漸地伸直了腰
來抵抗初雪的另一次壓倒」

When she suggested: "Leave some for robins"
Suddenly, to the sky the branches fling

A wasp circled and circled around my head
As if she warned us of something ahead
I responded: "It is all right, we don't need a ladder
And do leave some for squirrels and children later —
Do not ruin their world by our free will!
Besides, let the tree gradually straight up and grow
To fight for another bent by early snow."

路旁的知更

一隻褐腹的知更
在路旁啄一條蚯蚓
我走過時她只抬一抬頭
不願放棄她的戰利品

我下意識地拍一拍手
她只是倒退了幾寸
似乎不甘放掉她的美味
重拍時，她才直飛樹頂

我不知為甚要如此
和她去計較或相爭
這可能是人類的優越感
做什麼事都恣意任性

後來，我到遠處窺探
她會不會回來找尋？
也許，她已不齒我的作為
讓我的歉意，無處可申

A Roadside Robin

A robin with a brown belly
Was pecking a worm on a roadside
When I passed by she only looked up briefly
Unwilling to give up her captive easily

I clapped my hands subconsciously
She stepped back a few inches only
As if she would not abandon her delicacy
Until I clapped loudly, then she flew away

I do not know why I should do this
To compete or just to make a fuss
Could it be due to our human superiority
That we do whatever we please

Then I hide myself afar and peep
Will she come back again to seek?
I am afraid she has already despised me
And let my regrets have nowhere to speak

誤　會

我去花園中照料玫瑰
一隻黃蜂兒猛地向我衝來
好像非常憤怒、他向我示威
這是他的領域、豈容侵犯？

我不是存心去冒犯
他那塊丁點兒的天地
而且，花是我親手所栽
他豈能領會我的好意？

這樣的誤會、常充斥於天地之間
不去惹他、盼他今後會容忍一點

A Misunderstanding

I went to the garden to care for my roses

When a wasp headed forcefully in my way

Appearing very angry, he showed me his forces

And declared his territory: Nobody should invade

I did not intend to encroach or to offend

His tiny piece of private land

Besides, I myself planted these roses

My good intention does he understand?

This kind of misunderstanding is universally common

Ignoring him, I hope he will be tolerant from now on

詮　釋

玫瑰詮釋了夏季
岩石詮釋了愛情
流水詮釋了歲月
死亡詮釋了生命

詩，詮釋了我自己*

*這首小詩，寫在我出版的一首
　自傳性抒情長詩：《折扇》之前（2010）

Illustrations

Roses illustrate Summer

Rocks illustrate love

Flowing water illustrates time

Death illustrates life

And poetry, illustrates myself*

*This poem was written just before the publishing of
  my long autobiographical poem: "The Folding Fan" 2010

海灘的回憶

那年我們在一片沙灘上
留下了一頁落日的回憶
我們的足跡被淹沒千萬次
只有風一如往昔

在這片無常的地帶
沒有什麼可以持久
馬鞍藤昨日還爬得高興
今朝卻一無蹤影
白砂丘也似一群鴿子
被晚風逐得無痕

遠處的岩石似陸地的腳趾
在試探海潮起伏的感情
而海，總是浩浩地無邊
像死亡一樣肯定

夾在陸地和海洋之間
一切是短暫和多變

The Memory of a Beach

That year we came to this beach and we left

With a lasting memory of the sunset

Our footsteps were washed away million times

Only the wind is still the same

On this ever-changing sand strip

Nothing could really last long

Yesterday the morning glory was thriving

This morning they have already gone

White dunes like a flock of doves

Were swept clean by the evening cyclone

A distant rock, as a toe of the earth

Is testing the undulating emotions of the sea

And the sea, always vast and no end

Just like death, appears so sure to me

Existing between the sea and the land

All seem temporary and prone to change

一隻小蟹努力地爬上來
幾番、被浪潮退還
它給了我一點什麼啟示？
到如今不能忘懷

A little crab struggling to craw up shore

Was many times brought back by the tide

Up to this day I still could not forget

What a hint the little crab has left ?

美

我常想捕捉一種天然的美
鳶飛魚躍或澗水淙淙
用文字捉到後總覺得乏味
像流螢納入了瓶中

The Beauty of Nature

I always want to catch the beauty of nature

Eagles' soaring, fish's surfing, or creeks' singing

When it is captured in words I find no pleasure

Like fireflies caught in a bottle, disappointing

與佛勞斯特同坐

2010年6月底，得緣參觀丹佛市的Colorado Academy，
邂逅一尊詩人Robert Frost的坐像。起初我恭立在旁，後
來坐在他身邊，發現他手中寫的是名詩 "The Road Not
Taken"（未竟的路）。攝影留念，並誌其事

五十年前好友送給我，你的簽名集
珍藏迄今。過了兩年我造訪華盛頓
聽說你每一次從鄉下進京
那座五百呎的高塔也點頭致敬

我讀過、譯過、也宣揚過你的作品
嚮往一生。卻從未和你如此接近
現在可以擁抱你，和你並肩而坐
可以面詢你詩中的暗喻和象徵

你老當益壯，曾寫詩調侃死亡
在這裡你卻如此地瀟灑和年輕

Sitting with Robert Frost

Last June (2010) I had a chance to visit Colorado Academy
of Denver and encountered a sitting statue of Robert Frost. At
first, I stood there to pay my respect and then I sat by his side
and noticed that he was writing his famous poem: "The Road
Not taken."

Fifty years ago a friend gave me a signed copy of your anthology
That I've treasured it. Two years later I visited Washington D.C.
And I heard that every time you came to the nation's capital
The five hundred foot monument would nod and bow to thee

I have read, translated, and introduced your work all along
And respected you all my life. Yet I've never been so close to you
Now, I can hug you, rub shoulders with you, and ask you
In person, about the meaning of metaphors, symbols and so on

You wrote vigorously at your old age and even mocked Death
But here you are, looking so young, cool and elegant

我想：詩人不會老去，只是退隱
離世時還帶了一顆童真的心

現在我們倆緊緊地靠在一起
你聽到我的心跳，我看你握筆凝神
不一刻我們就東西睽離，只留下
一個永恆的你，和幾張攝影

今朝我未曾好好地準備和梳理
忽在此和你邂逅，感到靦腆和不敬
在你的面前，我和我的詩都似你所說
像剛出土的馬鈴薯，生澀而未洗淨

你是不朽的青銅，我乃漸衰的肉身
一株東方的水仙，一尊詩國的永恆
你曾感嘆: 有一條叉路，未曾走過
我因同時走兩條：一條也未走成

That makes me think: Poets never die, they only retreat
Even at death, they carry with them a young and innocent heart

Now we are sitting so closely to each other. You can feel
My heart beat and I watch you, pen in hand, with a intent look
After a short while we will depart. What will remain is
An eternal you and a few photos in my picture book

This morning I have neither dressed up nor prepared for
Our encountering here. I feel uneasy, disrespect and rude
In front of you, both myself and my poems are like nothing
But raw and un-cleaned potatoes, as you once alluded

You are an immortal bronze and I, a flesh becoming weakened
An oriental daffodil set against an eternity in the poetic kingdom
You have lamented that there was a road not taken
I took two roads simultaneously, neither one was successfully done

我不知道

為什麼要寫詩？我不知道
鳥為什麼要飛？雲為什麼
要飄？春天為什麼又來到？

我不知道，為什麼要寫詩？
是排遣冬日懨懨的無聊
或是，為我的存在寫照？

為什麼要寫照？我也不知道
也許，存在就是要不斷創造：
上帝的新葉子，我的新詩

從周遭冷冷厚厚的雪地裡
我的一股按捺不住的詩意
像鬱金香頂出了凍泥

I Don't Know

Why do I write poetry? I don't know
Why do clouds float and bird sing
And why every year back comes Spring?

I don't know, why do I write poetry?
Just for killing the dull Winter day
Or, to prove my existence in some way?

Why do I prove my existence, I don't know
Probably, existence requires endless creation:
As God's fresh leaves; so do my new poems

In the cold and heavy snow fields
My budding inspirations can't be suppressed
Like tulips' cracking the frozen ground

選　擇

一株黃鉛筆
如此凸顯
在下午陰暗的書房
當昏鴉在榆樹上喚不回
西沉的太陽

我像拾回了一株鏢箭
投向靈感的中央
聞到遠山的消息
那是久違的松香
那新出土的嫩尖
有一種蠢動的天機
忽然，使我眼睛發亮

我曾經陪伴它一段段
的歲月，短短長長
我的喜歡和憂傷
假如我必須選擇
寧願放棄現代的鍵盤
作原始和浪漫的一握

A Choice

A yellow pencil
Appeared so outstandingly
In my darkening study one evening
When a crow on the elm could not call back
The setting sun

I seem to have picked up a spear
That I can throw it at the center of inspiration
I can smell a message from the distant mountain
That was the pine fragrance long forgotten
Its earth-breaking tender tip
Has an impulse from the Heaven
Suddenly, my eyes start to gleam

I have accompanied it with many segments
Of my life, whether it was long or short
It witnessed my sorrows and happiness
If I have to make a choice
I would rather abandon my modern keyboard
For a primitive and romantic hold

簷　滴

有一種語言
勝過鄉音
使你聞之淚下
從這個世界
回到另一個

家是一個──
當聽到簷滴
就會使你
酸鼻的地方

Dripping from the Eaves

There is a kind of speech
Sweeter than one's native accent
When you hear it you will shed tears
And return from this world
Back to the one you came from

Home is the place —
Wherever you hear
Dripping from the eaves
Your nose feels burning and welling up

蜂　鳥

在光影幽微的外太空
一個纖小的造物時浮時沉
仰泳著宇宙的磁風
舞動剛健的雙翼和雄心

自五彩的太空站獲取補給
以長長弧管的一吸
也不時被那些衛星所激動——
營營的蜂群和嗡嗡甲蟲

無人知道它為什麼飛拍不停
不斷冒險豈造成真正的生靈？

Humming Bird

Under the twilight of the outer space
A small creature hardly keeps up his race
Floating and swimming against the solar wind
With his vibrating wings and strong mind

He gets from colorful stations his supplies
With a long, curved pipe-like beak
Occasionally he is annoyed by the satellites —
The buzzing bees and an ever-rushing bug

Nobody knows why he seldom stopped flying
Does endless adventure make a real Being?

年　老

一本書高擱以後
不知要到哪天才找獲

拉起弓射出之前
找不到標的，也丟失了箭

聽風在林梢穿過
便隨著它，出神去遠

看夕陽落海的美景
卻仰慕一顆顫顫的黃昏星

Old Age

After a book is shelved
Who knows when he will again find

When a bow is drawn
He forgets targets, and loses his arrow

Hearing the wind combs the forest
He is carried away and drafts his thought

Facing a wonderful scene of sunset
He admires a flickering evening star, instead

黃　昏

一隻巨鷹向西天撲去
如夸父般地追蹤
也許它只想探一顆星
或為了一片霞紅

而海，這時已經半醺
泛出了酡紅的臉龐
不能忍受熾熱的一吻
退隱在夜幕後方

這是一幅亙古的動畫
過往的人都會矚目
多看一眼不算是貪婪
一生有幾回駐足？

人都說：夕陽無限好
只是留不住餘輝
且回去將它認真捕捉
不悲落日和年歲

At Dusk

A huge eagle dashes to the west sky
Like Kua-fu, ever chasing of the sun*
He may only want to search for a star
Or, for the cloud's rosy attraction

Now, the sea looks half-drunk
A red flush has appeared on her cheek
She can not bear the hot kiss from the sun
And retreats behind the night's curtain

This is an eternal picture of animation
Whoever passes-by would stand and stare
One more look is not a greedy action
In your life how many stops have you taken?

A setting sun is a boundless beauty, they say
Yet, no one can make it really stay
I'll bring it home and capture its image
With no lament and complaint of my age

---

* In Chinese myth, a man called Kua-fu chases the sun all the time. Also, a Chinese saying: "The setting sun is a boundless beauty. Alas, it is near the dusk."

我的遺願

請不要讓我
躺在狹窄的空間
　　聽不到畫眉的細語
　　嗅不到茉莉的清香
讓我飛揚
在雄偉的河谷之上
疲倦了，像隻鷹
棲息在岩石的山頂
瞰視天地和東方

請不要置我在
天平之上
用 $ 來斤斤計量
我願意夾在
舊書店的木架上
讓人們翻閱、瀏覽
當他們飢於詩
　　　渴於愛
卻只有兩只
空空的口袋

My Last Will

Do not let me, please
Lie in a confined space
   To hear no song of thrush
    And smell no aroma of jasmine
Please let me fly high
And over a grand valley
When tired, I rest like an eagle
Atop a bare rock peak
And overlook the world and the East

Please do not place me
On a delicate scale
And use $ to weigh my value
I would like to be squeezed
At a shelf in a used-book store
And let people take a glance or read
When they are hungry for poems
    Or thirsty for love
Even when all that they have
Are two empty pockets

對不起，上帝
請不要拘我在天堂
或向那地獄釋放
（在世時，我慣於
跋涉四方）
請給我一具宇宙的GPS
　　讓我去黑洞探險
　　任我在銀河徜徉

Sorry, God

Please do not detain me in Heaven

Or set me free to Hell

(In this world, I am accustomed

To roaming around the Earth)

So please give me a universal GPS

    Let me explore a black hole

    Let me wander in the galaxy

墓誌銘

這裡躺著一個詩人
沒有桂冠，沒沒無聞
此刻他還在地下期待
繆斯最後的評定

Epitaph

Here lies a poet

Without fame, let alone a Laureate

Who is still awaiting underground

The Muse's final judgment

瞬間的浩劫
──寫在四川二○○八年五月十二日 大地震後五天

山搖地撼
石破天驚
這瞬間的板塊移位
使全球震駭、上蒼落淚

母親捨命保女嬰
留言：記住，我愛你
學童截肢保性命
哀求：留隻寫字的右手
如此悽慘的一幕幕
不忍想、也不忍睹

對大自然的浩劫
無法預告、感到無奈
我們雖然常常自豪
一秒鐘可以計算幾兆

Catastrophes in a Minute
The Sichuan May 12, 2008 Earthquake, China

Mountains swayed, earth quivered

Sky shook and rocks shattered

Only in a minute, the crushed earth plates

Shocked the entire world and made heaven wept

Shielding an infant daughter, a dying mother

Left a note: Do remember, I love you

A rescued school boy in need of amputation

Begged: Keep my right hand for writing

So sadly, one scene after another

I could not bear to watch, let alone to think

Facing this magnitude of catastrophe

There was no warning. We felt totally helpless

Though we are always proud of our speed

Of calculation, hundred million times a second

不忍想、也不忍睹
這致命的三天已過
在我們血濃於水的內心
無時無刻不在關懷
這些日漸微弱的呻吟
雖在千里以外

I could not bear to watch, let alone to think

The deadly-three-days have now passed

Yet, in our heart, blood is thicker than water

Not a minute has passed we stopped listening

To the gradually diminished groaning of many*

Though they are thousand miles away

*The poem was written at the fifth day after the quake.

聽海
──一隻海螺的獨白

你們為什麼要來聽海？
為了如鼓如風、澎湃的潮音
那種令人奮發、鼓舞的天籟

你們為什麼要來聽海？
為了日以繼夜、柔柔的浪聲
那種永恆的耳語和關愛

這些都是，也都不是
我要傾聽的是大地的跫音
　　發自地軸的輪轉
　　起自千里的風雲
　　來自滿月的呼應

我是貼在海涯沙灘上的
　　一隻詩人的耳朵

Listen to the Sea
A Monolog of a Conch

Why do you come to listen to the sea?
Is it for its roaring sound, like wind and drum
Nature's music that excites and exhilarates you?

Why do you come to listen to the sea?
Is it for its everlasting melodies, soft and peaceful
A kind of eternal whispers and love?

All these are reasons, yet they are not
What I want to listen are Earth's footsteps
     Its rhythms from rotating axis
     Its sounds from gathering wind and clouds
     And its reactions to the full moon

Lying flat on a beach far away
     I am the ear of a poet

對流
CONVECTION

第二輯：中譯
——夏菁譯英美詩人的詩

Part Two: Chinese Translations
Author's Translations of English poems into Chinese

與佛勞斯特同坐　Sitting with Robert Frost

佛勞斯特（Robert Frost）

　　佛勞斯特（1874-1963）是美國近代大詩人之一。他的詩很受大眾喜愛，而且廣為引用。他的詩作，大多以新英格蘭的農村生活為背景，但詩中含有的社會意識、人性、以及哲理，卻是世界性的。佛勞斯特一生，曾得過四次普立茲詩獎及無數榮譽。

　　Robert Frost (1874-1963) was one of the great American poets in recent history. His works are very popular and often quoted. He wrote mostly under the background of rural life in New England, yet his poems contain the universal social, humane and philosophical implications. During his lifetime, he received four Pulitzer Prizes of poetry and numerous honors.

Stopping by Woods on a Snowy Evening

Whose woods these are I think I know.
His house is in the village though;
He will not see me stopping here
To watch his woods fill up with snow.

My little horse must think it queer
To stop without a farmhouse near
Between the woods and frozen lake
The darkest evening of the year.

He gives his harness bells a shake
To ask if there is some mistake.
The only other sound's the sweep
Of easy wind and downy flake.

The woods are lovely, dark and deep.
But I have promises to keep,
And miles to go before I sleep,
And miles to go before I sleep.

雪夜林畔

我想我知道這是誰的森林。
他的家雖在那邊鄉村；
他看不到我駐足在此地
佇望他的森林白雪無垠。

我的小馬一定會覺得離奇
停留於曠無農舍之地
在這森林和冰湖的中間
一年內最昏暗的冬夕。

它將它的佩鈴朗朗一牽
問我有沒有弄錯了地點。
此外但聞微風的拂吹
和紛如鵝毛的雪片。

這森林真可愛、黝黑而深邃。
可是我還要去趕赴約會，
還要趕好幾哩路才安睡，
還要趕好幾哩路才安睡。

Looking for a Sunset Bird in Winter

The west was getting out of gold,

The breath of air had died of cold,

When shoeing home across the white,

I thought I saw a bird alright.

In summer when I passed the place

I had to stop and lift my face;

A bird with an angelic gift

Was singing in it sweet and swift.

No bird was singing in it now.

A single leaf was on a bough,

And that was all there was to see

In going twice around the tree.

From my advantage on a hill

I judged that such a crystal chill

Was only adding frost to snow

As gilt to gold that wouldn't show.

冬夕望鳥歸

西天的金色已漸漸暗隱，
大氣也在嚴寒中僵凝，
當我踏上歸途、橫跨雪地，
我想我見到一隻小鳥棲息。

夏季每當我徒步過此
我習於止步、仰首凝視；
一隻小鳥具有天使的聲音
正在枝頭作甜脆的囀鳴。

現在沒有小鳥在樹端歌唱。
僅有枯葉一枚殘留枝上，
所能目睹的也只此一點
當我繞樹兩匝別無所見。

我借著小山俯覽之際
審度這般透明的寒氣
不過像雪上加了層霜
了無痕跡、好比鍍金於金上。

A brush had left a crooked stroke
Of what was either cloud or smoke
From north to south across the blue;
A piercing little star was through.

一抹畫筆現剩下彎曲一線
像是晚霞又好似暮煙
從北而南橫展在藍天之上；
一顆刺透的寒星已熠熠發光。

A Minor Bird

I have wished a bird would fly away,
And not sing by my house all day;

Have clapped my hands at him from the door
When it seemed as if I could bear no more.

The fault must partly have been in me.
The bird was not to blame for his key.

And of course there must be something wrong
In wanting to silence any song.

小 鳥

我曾經盼望過一隻鳥飛掉，
不要整日價在屋旁鳴叫；

也曾在門口對著他拍掌作聲
當我似乎是不能再容忍。

這種過失一部份在於我自己。
小鳥的聲調原無可非議。

要教任何歌都不許唱，
這種想法本身就是狂妄。

In Hardwood Groves

The same leaves over and over again!
They fall from giving shade above,
To make one texture of faded brown
And fit the earth like a leather glove.

Before the leaves can mount again
To fill the trees with another shade,
They must go down past things coming up.
They must go down into the dark decayed.

They must be pierced by flowers and put
Beneath the feet of dancing flowers,
However it is in some other world
I know that this is the way in ours.

闊葉林中

同樣的枯葉愈積愈多！
都落自頂上的綠蔭，
給地面敷上一層枯黃
像皮手套那樣配稱。

在新葉能夠繁生以前
為樹木長成另一個華蓋，
這些枯葉必定要遭到輪迴，
必定落入了黑沉沉的朽敗。

它們一定會被花芽頂穿
並置身於她歡樂的足畔。
雖然這是在另一個世界
我知道我們的也是一般。

Spring Pools

These pools that, though in forests, still reflect

The total sky almost without defect,

And like the flowers beside them, chill and shiver,

Will like the flowers beside them soon be gone,

And yet not out by any brook or river,

But up by roots to bring dark foliage on.

The trees that have it in their pent-up buds

To darken nature and be summer woods —

Let them think twice before use their powers

To blot out and drink up and sweep away

These flowery waters and these watery flowers

From snow that melted only yesterday.

春天的池沼

這些池沼，雖然在森林之中
仍能完美的反映天空，
它們像池邊的花般、凜冽顫抖，
也將如身畔的花朵瞬即消逝，
現在尚未注入任何小溪或河流，
只沿樹根而上，將濃葉蕃孳。

含在樹木鬱積待放的嫩芽裡
發為陰陰夏木，遮蔽天地——
讓它們在施展力量前再三想過，
然後去吸乾、飲盡以及消除
這些如花的池水以及如水的花朵
僅僅自昨日的雪內融出。

In a Disused Graveyard

The living come with grassy tread
To read the gravestones on the hill;
The graveyard draws the living still,
But never any more the dead.

The verses in it say and say:
"The ones who living come today
To read the stones and go away
Tomorrow dead will come to stay."

So sure of death the marbles rhyme,
Yet can't help marking all the time
How no one dead will seem to come,
What is it men are shrinking from?

It would be easy be clever
And tell the stones: Men hate to die
And have stopped dying now forever.
I think they would believe the lie.

廢　墓

生者踐踏著荒草前來，
到山上瀏覽墓石的碑文；
這廢墓仍然吸引著生人，
對死者則已無奈。

墓地到處是類似的韻文：
「今天你們活著而來的人
讀罷碑文然後回程
明白謝世將來此葬身。」

對死亡如此肯定、這些碑碣，
現在卻不得不常常注意及
為何死了的不再到此安歇，
人們為什麼又畏縮不前？

我們很可以變得俏皮
對墓石說：人類對死亡已厭，
且已永生不死，從現在起。
我想它們會信此謊言。

A Peck of Gold

Dust always blowing about the town,
Except when sea-fog laid it down,
And I was one of the children told
Some of the blowing dust was gold.

All the dust the wind blew high
Appeared like gold in the sunset sky,
But I was one of the children told
Some of the dust was really gold.

Such was life in the Golden Gate:
Gold dusted all we drank and ate,
And I was one of the children told,
"We all must eat our peck of gold."

黃金的灰塵

塵埃常在城市的四周飛揚，
除非有海霧將它壓降，
我是孩童中聽說過的一人
有些飛揚的塵埃原是黃金。

所有的塵土被風兒高高吹起
一望如金、在落日的天際，
但我是孩童中聽說過的一人
有些塵土是實實在在的黃金。

像我們置身在黃金的國門*：
吃喝全離不了黃金的灰塵，
我曾是孩童中聽說過的一人，
「一生必定要飽嘗黃金的灰塵。」

* Golden Gate原是指金門橋及其海灣一帶，詩人曾住過舊金山多年，這是一個雙關
  語；因舊金山曾是淘金之地，又是美國西岸的入口。

Nothing Gold can Stay

Nature's first green is gold,

Her hardest hue to hold.

Her early leaf's a flower;

But only so an hour.

Then leaf subsides to leaf.

So Eden sank to grief,

So dawn goes down to day.

Nothing gold can stay.

黃金時代不久留

大自然的新綠呈金黃色，
這是最不能持久者。
她初生的樹葉像花兒一朵：
何奈其瞬息即過。
然後是落英的繽紛。
伊甸園淪為愁城，
黎明降成了白晝。
黃金時代不久留。

對流
CONVECTION

勞倫斯（D.H. Lawrence）

　　勞倫斯（1885-1930）是近代的英國詩人、小說家、和批評家。他一生寫了八百首詩和出版了大約十本詩集。當他開始寫詩時，「意象派」還有待具體的表現；他對意象派出版的選集貢獻很大。後來，勞倫斯作了比意象派更進一步的改革，寫出易懂的詩，且可立即扣人心弦。他的詩有很大部份是自由詩。有些論者認為他的詩可躋身於廿世紀最重要的作品，與艾略特和葉慈的詩並駕齊驅。他對大西洋兩岸的很多現代詩人，具有顯著的影響。

　　D.H. Lawrence (1885-1930), an English poet, novelist, and critic, produced about eight hundred poems during his lifetime and published some ten volumes of poetry. Lawrence began writing poetry at the time when "Imagism" was seeking more concrete expression. He contributed considerably to Imagist Anthologies. Later on, Lawrence took a revolution further than the Imagists, writing accessible poetry that was immediately appealing. A great number of his poems were free verse. Some critics view his poetry as among the most important produced in the 20th Century, deserving to be set alongside with the work of T.S. Eliot and W.B. Yeats. He had significant influences on many contemporary poets on both sides of the Atlantic.

After the Opera

Down the stone stairs
Girls with their large eyes wide with tragedy
Lift looks of shocked and momentous emotion up at me.
And I smile.

Ladies
Stepping like birds with their bright and pointed feet
Peer anxiously forth, as if for a boat to carry them out of wreckage;
And among the wreck of the theatre crowd
I stand and smile.
They take tragedy so becomingly;
Which pleases me.

But when I meet the weary eyes
The reddened, aching eyes of the bar-man with thin arms,
I am glad to go back to where I came from.

歌劇散場

走下石級
女孩們以充滿悲劇的大眼
激動和嚴重地抬頭望著我。
我微笑。

仕女們
以尖細光滑之足像小鳥般走下
向前急切張望，如盼望一艘船前來搭救；
在這些沉船的觀眾之間
我站著而且微笑。
他們如此地易於接受悲劇
使我覺得好笑。

但當我遇到一雙疲睏的眼睛
一雙酒保紅紅的、痛苦的眼睛和他羸弱的手臂時，
我樂於回到我來的地方去。

The White Horse

The youth walks up to the white horse, to put its halter on
And the horse looks at him in silence.
They are so silent they are in another world.

白　馬

那青年走到白馬旁，將韁繩套上
這匹馬靜靜地望著他
他們是如此靜謐，他們在另一個世界裡

The Mosquito Knows

The mosquito knows full well, small as he is

he's a beast of prey.

But after all

he only takes his bellyful,

he doesn't put my blood in the bank.

蚊蟲知道

蚊蟲知道得很清楚，他雖然小
卻是一個食肉獸。
但究竟
他只裝滿自己的肚腹，
並未將我的血存入銀行。

The Gods! The Gods!

People were bathing, and posturing themselves on the beach
and all was dreary, great robot limbs, robot breasts
robot voices, robot even the gay umbrellas.

But a woman, shy and alone, was washing herself under a tap
and the glimmer of the presence of the gods was like lilies,
and like water-lilies.

神！神！

人們在水邊沐浴，在沙灘上忸怩作態
全是乏味的機械人的四肢，機械人的乳房
機械人的聲音，甚至花洋傘也是。

可是一個含羞和孤獨的女人，在水龍頭下洗滌
在幽微光影中顯身的神祇像百合，
像水仙。

A White Blossom

A tiny moon as small and white as a single jasmine flower

Leans all alone above my window, on night's wintry bower,

Liquid as lime-tree blossom, soft as brilliant water or rain

She shines, the first white love of my youth, passionless and in vain.

一朵白花

一個小小的月亮、皎潔玲瓏如一朵茉莉
孤單地斜依在我的窗上，在這冬晚的寢室裡，
澄澈如檸檬的花朵，柔和像燦爛的水或雨珠
它照耀著我潔白的初戀，無情且無果。

Humming Bird

I can imagine, in some otherworld
Primeval-dumb, far back
In that most awful stillness, that only gasped and hummed,
Humming-birds raced down the avenues.

Before anything had a soul,
While life was a heave of Matter, half inanimate,
This little bit chipped off in brilliance
And went whizzing through the slow, vast, succulent stems.

I believe there were no flowers then,
In the world where the humming-bird flashed ahead of creation.
I believe he pierced the slow vegetable veins with his long beak.

Probably he was big
As mosses, and little lizards they say, were once big.
Probably he was a jabbing, terrifying monster.
We look at him through the wrong end of the telescope of Time,
Luckily for us.

蜂　鳥

我能想見，在太古般沉寂的
另一個天地，遠遠地
在最最的靜謐裡，只有喘息和營營的
蜂鳥們競奔於林蔭道間。

在萬物具有靈魂之前，
生命還是一團混沌的物質，一半還沒有生氣，
這個在光耀奪目中剝落的小角色
已衝刺於生長緩慢、碩大、多汁的莖間。

我相信那時還沒有花朵，
在那個天地裡，蜂鳥閃現於一切造物之前。
我相信他用長長的喙，啄穿慢慢延伸的葉脈。

也許，他只像
苔蘚那麼大，小蜥蜴，據說曾經很大。
也許他是一隻猛擊的可怖的巨獸。

我們從時間望遠鏡的錯誤的一端望他，
我們夠幸運。

Prayer

Give the moon at my feet
Put my feet upon the crescent, like a Lord!
O let my ankles be bathed in moonlight, that I may go
sure and moon-shoed, cool and bright-footed
towards my goal.

For the sun is hostile, now
his face is like the red lion,
...

祈禱者

給我以月，在腳邊
置我的雙足於半鉤新月之上，像一個主宰！
啊，讓我的足踝沐浴於月光之中，我可以
坦然前行，穿著月鞋、涼爽光鮮地
走向我的目的地。

因為太陽是有敵意的，現在
他的臉如一頭紅獅，
……

Search for Love

Those that go searching for love
only make manifest their own lovelessness,
and the loveless never find love,
only the loving find love,
and they never have to seek for it.

尋　愛

那些尋愛的人
只是在昭告自己沒有愛心，
沒有愛心的人永遠找不到愛，
只有，有愛心的人才找得到愛，
他們卻從不需要去找尋。

Nothing to Save

There is nothing to save, now all is lost,
but a tiny core of stillness in the heart
like the eye of a violet.

無可挽救

無可挽救，現在全部已失去，
僅有一丁點的沉靜在心中
像紫羅蘭的新芽。

Self-Pity

I never saw a wild thing

sorry for itself.

A small bird will drop frozen dead from a bough

without ever having felt sorry for itself.

自　憐

我從未見到野生的東西
會自怨自憐。
一隻小鳥將從枝頭凍斃跌下來
他未曾為自己感到可憐。

對流
CONVECTION

浩司曼（A.E. Housman）

　　浩司曼（1859-1936），英國詩人兼古典拉丁文學者，曾任倫敦及劍橋大學教授。他一生出版過二本著名的詩集：《夏洛普郡的少年》和《最後的詩篇》。他的詩頗受莎士比亞詩歌、德國詩人海涅、以及蘇格蘭民謠的影響。他主張詩應避開思想，直追感情。

　　A.E. Housman (1859-1936), an English poet and classical scholar in Latin, was a professor at London University and Cambridge. He published two famed books in poetry: *A Shropshire Lad* and *Last Poems*. His poems were influenced by the songs of Shakespeare, Heinrich Heine, and the Scottish Border Ballads. He claimed that poetry should bypass thought, and plunge to the very pit of emotion.

Loveliest of Trees

Loveliest of trees, the cherry now
Is hung with bloom along the bough,
And stands about the woodland ride
Wearing white for Eastertide.

Now, of my threescore years and ten,
Twenty will not come again,
And take from seventy springs a score,
It only leaves me fifty more.

And since to look at things in bloom
Fifty springs are little room,
About the woodlands I will go
To see the cherry hung with snow.

心愛的樹

心愛的樹，這櫻桃
正開滿了花，沿著枝條，
玉立亭亭地在林道旁
為復活節穿上潔白的衣裳。

人生只不過七十歲，
雙十年華，一去不復回，
從七十裡減掉二十個春季，
僅能剩給我五十而已。

看盛開的花，如火如荼
五十季實嫌短促，
因此我還是去樹林內
看櫻花與雪同輝。

When I was One-and-Twenty

When I was one-and-twenty
I heard a wise man say,
"Give crowns and pounds and guineas
But not your heart away;
Give pearls away and rubies
But Keep your fancy free."
But I was one-and-twenty,
No use to talk to me.

When I was one-and-twenty
I heard him say again,
"The heart out of the bosom
Was never given in vain;
It's paid with sighs a plenty
And sold for endless rue."
And I am two-and-twenty,
And oh, 'tis true, 'tis true.

當我是二十有一

當我是二十有一
我聽到智者說起，
「你可以將錢財散盡
但不要將心丟棄；
你可割捨珍珠寶石
但要保存好你的遐思。」
但我是二十有一，
聽不進這種言詞。

當我是二十有一
我聽到他又說一回，
「這個在胸中的心臟
獻出去不會白費；
它值得很多的嘆息
無盡的悲傷是代價。」
我現在是二十有二，
啊！不假，不假。

對流
CONVECTION

戴維斯（W.H. Davies）

戴維斯（1871-1940）1871年生於英國的南威爾斯。兩歲喪父，母也棄他而去。他十餘歲即輟學，從事學徒及零工。廿二歲到北美流浪六年，直到在加拿大失去一足才回國。回倫敦以後，他從事寫詩。在1905年34歲時才出版第一本詩集；一生出版有十六本之多。所寫多以大自然為主題，風格簡約樸實，享譽及風行一時，深受蕭伯納的青睞。戴維斯歿於1940年。

W.H. Davies was born in South Wales, 1871. He was abandoned by his mother at two when his father died. He left school in his teen years and worked as apprentice and laborer. At age 22, he traveled to America for six years as tramp until he lost his foot in Canada. In returning to London he devoted himself to writing. His first collection of poems was published in 1905 at the age of 34. Throughout his lifetime, he published sixteen books of poems. Most of his poetry surrounds the subject of nature and exhibits simplicity and earthy style. His poems were once quite popular and received high praise from Bernard Shaw. He died at 1940.

Leisure

What is this life if, full of care,
We have no time to stand and stare —

No time to stand beneath the boughs,
And stare as long as sheep and cows:

No time to see, when woods we pass,
Where squirrels hide their nuts in grass:

No time to see, in broad daylight,
Streams full of stars, like skies at night:

No time to turn at Beauty's glance,
And watch her feet, how they can dance:

No time to wait till her mouth can
Enrich that smile her eyes began.

A poor life this if, full of care,
We have no time to stand and stare.

閒　暇

這是什麼生活，戰戰兢兢，
我們若沒有時間去凝視、站定——

沒有時間在樹下小傍，
像牛羊一般地出神癡望：

沒有時間探視路邊的樹林，
有松鼠把乾果在草間藏隱：

沒有時間欣賞晴朗的白晝中，
小溪充滿閃爍、猶如夜空：

沒有時間領會美的盼顧，
注意她的腳、怎樣婆娑起舞：

沒有時間等待她嫣然一笑
當她的眼中透露了先兆。

如此可憐的生活，戰戰兢兢，
我們若沒有時間去凝視、站定。

The Example

Here's an example from
A Butterfly
That on a rough, hard rock
Happy can lie;
Friendless and all alone
On this unsweetened stone.

Now let my bed be hard
No care take I;
I'll make my joy like this
Small Butterfly;
Whose happy heart has power
To make a stone a flower.

榜　樣

這裡有一個榜樣：
一隻蝴蝶
在粗糙堅硬的岩盤上
快樂也能棲息；
孤獨而缺乏友情
在這冷漠的石頂。

現在，任我的床再堅硬
我也不關心；
和那隻小蝴蝶一樣
我歡樂自尋；
它的樂觀能功奪造化
使頑石變成鮮花。

My Youth

My youth was my old age,
Weary and long;
It had too many cares
To think of song;
My moulting days all came
When I was young.

Now, in life's prime, my soul
Comes out in flower;
Late, as with Robin, comes
My singing power;
I was not born to joy
Till this late hour.

我的青春時代

我的青春是我的老年，
疲乏又漫長；
那時有太多的憂慮
想不到要歌唱；
我衰頹和慘綠的日子
都在年輕時光。

如今到盛年，我的心靈
自花朵中躍升；
遲緩地像知更鳥一般
歌唱的力量萌生；
我原不是生下來就歡樂
直到過了大半生。

對流
CONVECTION

第三輯：友譯
——友人英譯夏菁的詩

Part Three: Friends' Translations
Friends' Translations of Hsia Ching's Poems into English

羅馬街頭的噴泉　A Fountain in Rome

譯者簡介 Translator

王季文（**C.W. Wang**）

王季文，1924年生於江蘇昆山。1949年畢業於英國皇家海軍學校，在臺灣服役海軍二十餘年至艦長級退役。1970年後，在高雄加工出口區任職，直到1989年二次退休。在他眾多的翻譯作品中，晚近的有《宋詞英譯》（臺灣皇冠出版社出版）和《滕王閣序》等。他現居加州。

C.W. Wang was born in Jiangsu in 1924. A 1949 graduate from the British Royal Naval School, he served in the Navy in Taiwan for two decades and retired at the rank of Captain. In 1970, he joined the Kaohsiung Export Processing Zone Administration until his second retirement in 1989. Among his many translations, the recent ones include 〝*Songs of Sung Dynasty*〞（宋詞英譯）and 〝*An Introduction to the Pavilion of Prince of Tang*〞（滕王閣序）. Wang is now living in California.

灰鯨落海
──悼二十世紀

龐然一擊
在暮色無邊之際
二十世紀的尾巴
若灰鯨的落海

浪花四濺
如歷史的爭紛
頃刻將歸入寧靜
不管是悲壯的號角
纏綿的往事
或苦難的呻吟

人類的回憶
只是海上的晚風
現在，一切的一切
要看明日的光中

The Fall of a Grey Whale
In Memory of the 20th Century

A big bang following the mighty strike
In the boundless twilight of the Eve
The tail of the Twentieth Century, like
A grey whale falls back into the vast wave

Breaking billows splash in all directions
Like what happened in history: All commotions
Will soon return to serenity
Be it the trumpet of war and tragedy
An enduring romance in days of old
Or the groans of hunger and cold

The memory of human beings, you see
Is but an evening breeze over the sea
Now, all in all, we can only fix our sight
At a gleam of hope, in morn's dawning light

Translated by C.W. Wang

螺　音

地球的轉軸在孳孳發聲
前面還有億兆里路程
我的終站，也許就在
那邊望得見的海濱

像一隻刺鳥，還要唱歌
不管歌聲只迴盪於螺殼
喧嚷的大海將歌聲掩蓋
世紀的寒流呼嘯而過

隨你說：古調或是新潮
幾圈後我們都隨風飄渺
要等到有一天一雙慧耳
在螺殼中將歌詞找到

The Sound of a Shell

The earth's axis murmurs zzz zzz
Its journey ahead still has trillions of miles
Yet my own final destination will be
Perhaps, on that yonder beach you can see

Like a thorn bird I still need to sing
Although the voice echoes only in the shell
The roaring sea muffled my songs all the time
While century's cold fronts swept by whirring

Whatever you say: a classic tone or a modern song
A few revolving rounds, and we'll all be gone
And not until some day, someone with ears of magic
Will find in the shell the verse and music

Translated by C.W. Wang

四　月

「四月是最殘酷的月份」*
這話，我不會同意
復活節剛吹過百合的喇叭
積雪正寸寸撤離
櫻花的蓓蕾稚氣勃勃
鬱金香頂出凍泥
空中充滿了求偶的呼喚
沒有比四月更富生機

我坐擁四月乍暖的陽光
推不開這句詩的陰翳
鉤玄、織文、刻意的深奧
已演成數十年的積習
像我這種天性，自然純樸
對四月怎會不歡喜

*這句詩是美國近代著名詩人艾略特《荒原》中的第一句

April

"April is the cruellest month"*

This, I cannot agree with

The Easter lily just had its trumpets blown

Retreating inch by inch is the winter snow

And cherry buds are full of innocence

From frozen soils a tulip makes its appearance

The air is filled with mating calls

April is the nicest growing month after all

Sitting under the warmish April sunshine

I can't dispel the dark shadow left by this line

To bend on pursuing obscurity and difficulty

Had for decades grown to be a deep rooted habit

With a disposition akin to nature and simplicity

How can I not to love April dearly

Translated by C.W. Wang

*The first line in "The Waste Land," by T.S. Eliot.

羅　馬

1. 阿望鐵諾山

太陽從梵諦岡
後面的馬里奧山沉落
這裡就進入另一個世界

在Aventino的山崗
許多年輕的情侶
擁吻在石柱、鐘樓
赭色的垣牆旁
他們的旭日正在昇上

而我，保守的外邦人
踩著輕輕的腳步
忽然地也低哼
那首名曲: 我的太陽
——且情不自禁

Rome

1.Aventino

As the sun set down at Mt. Mario
Behind the City of Vatican
This place enters into another world

On the high grounds of Aventino
Many young lovers embrace
And kiss beside the stone pillars
Bell tower and red-brown walls
Their morning sun is now arising

As for me, a conservative stranger
Walking at a light-footed gait
Suddenly started to hum
The famous song: Sole Mio
— And felt an irresistible impulse

2. 鬥獸場

只有一簇簇的遊客
不見餓獅和受難的信徒
教皇在聖彼德安坐
這一切已成為陳跡

在金黃的夕照下
我猛一回頭
只見蝙蝠如黑胡椒一般
紛紛灑落在這塊
義大利的披薩之上

3. 摩西坐像

好像坐在這裡已經很久了
自從出了埃及

筋脈還是那麼脹起
長鬚在風中飄逸
還有眼神的關切

上帝只賜你一塊戒禁──
一雙巧手
卻賦你以永恆
用斧一把、鑿一柄

170

2.The Colosseum

There are only groups of tourists, and

No hungry lions and Christian martyrs in sight

The Pope is securely seated at the St. Peter's

All those things are now but relics

Under the golden sunset

As I suddenly turned my head

I saw masses of bats landing, like

Spreading of black pepper

Onto this giant piece of Pizza Italia

3.Statue of Moses

As if he's been sitting here for a long while

Since the Exodus

His veins are still swelling

Long beards flap in the air

And in his eyes there are love and care

God had given you only a plague —

Yet, a pair of dexterous hands

Had endowed you with eternity

By means of a chisel, an axe

4. 聖彼德教堂

踏著紫紅大理石的拼花
仰望圓頂雕繪的精細
心想，這般華麗和堂皇
可是上帝謙卑的原意？

走出宏偉的大門
有一群白鴿從地上驚起
那種單純和突然
使我受一次不期的洗禮

自從到過聖彼德以後
已無第二座可觀可比
倒是一個小小的土地廟
有時會引起我的好奇

4.At St. Peter's

Treading upon the red-purple patterned marble floor
Looking up at the dome's exquisite carvings and paintings
I wonder, how can this kind of splendor be
In line with God's teaching: Be humble?

Stepping out from that great door
I startled off, from the ground, a flock of doves
It was this kind of simplicity and abruptness
That I was unexpectedly baptized

Since I visited the grand St. Peter's
There will be none comparable to see
Yet, a tiny and insignificant Temple of Earth God
Did arouse, sometimes, my curiosity

5. Trevi 噴泉

傳說，丟進一個銅子
你可以再回羅馬一次
三十年前，我丟進幾枚
誰也不承認的鎳幣
倒也回去好幾次

在那時羅馬及全歐州
能待我以國際公平的
只有這座友好的噴泉

6. 羅馬古道

零落的石板道
凱撒駛過。安東尼追過
勃魯特斯遁過。時間溜過
兩千年來，風風雨雨

通到世界的盡頭
通過世紀的興衰
兩千年來，日出日落
歷史只不過是
兩排見證的古柏樹

5.Fountain Trevi

Legend says: Throw in a penny

Once again back to Rome you may

Thirty years ago I'd thrown in some nickels

Which was not recognized by any other countries

Yet, I did come back to Rome several times

In Rome, or in Europe at that time

No one treated us with diplomatic fairness

Except this friendly Fountain Trevi

6.An Ancient Track

On an ancient track with scattering slabs

Caesar drove past, Antonio pursued through

Brutus fled away, and time slipped by

In the past two thousand years, winds and storms

It led to the final destination of the world

And passed through ups and downs of the centuries

In the past two thousand years, sun rouse and sun set

History is but those two side-rows

Of age old, eye witnessing cypress

Translated by C.W. Wang

175

西湖、溫柔的眼神

西湖、溫柔的眼神
美目盼兮

千里迢迢
這種眼神，我知道
映在花港觀魚的水裡
藏在蘇堤的拱橋
隱隱約約，尋尋覓覓
暮暮朝朝

那種眼神，那種溫柔
只有在晨昏交替之際
山色有無之中
以及愛你的人一顰一笑
才能找得到

美目盼兮
雖然千里迢迢
你的眼神
我避不開，躲不了

The West Lake, a Tender Look in Eyes

The West Lake, a tender look in eyes
How beautiful is your charming glance

A thousand miles away, yet
This kind of look in eyes, I knew:
Reflects upon the water of "Hua Gang"
Hides at the arch bridge of Su Di*
Just visible, just obscured; for seek, for search
Day and night

That kind of look, that kind of tenderness
Only at when the night and day begin to alter
Only at when the mountain hue is uncertain
And when the loved one flashes a smile
That its presence I may find

How beautiful is your charming glance
Although it is a thousand miles apart
The very look in your eyes
I can not evade, can not escape

Translated by C.W. Wang

* Hua Gang and Su Di are the name of places. The former means floral cove and the latter,
  dyke built by Poet Su Dong Po.

對流
CONVECTION

譯者簡介 Translator
John J.S. Balcom（陶忘機）

John J.S. Balcom is a freelance writer, translator and Associate Professor and Head of the Chinese program of the Graduate School of Translation and Interpretation at the Monterey Institute of International Studies, California, USA. He earned his Ph.D. in Chinese and Comparative Literature from Washington University in St. Louis and has translated many contemporary Taiwanese poems into English.

陶忘機，美國人。一位自由作者及翻譯家。現為美國加州 Monterey Institute of International Studies的中文部主任及副教授。獲有聖路易斯華盛頓大學比較文學博士學位。曾譯過無數台灣詩人的現代詩成英文。

雪　嶺

一座潔白的雪嶺
常在我腦際浮現
不知是幻是真

在不可及的天邊
在晨昏的交替
在有無之間

是不是我的癡迷
或是你臥姿的誘人
揮不去、難忘記

有一座永恆
一片聖潔的誘惑
向我日夜招引

Snow Peak

A pure white snowy peak
Often appears in my mind
An illusion or real, I can't be sure

On the unattainable horizon
Where dawn and dusk cross
Between form and formlessness

Am I infatuated or
Is it your reposing seductiveness
Unforgettable, alluring

An eternal
Seduction of purity and holiness
Attracting me day and night

Translated by John J.S. Balcom

我們是湖

我們承載
自蘆葦和卵石間
流出、時間的長流
有錚錚作聲的屈原
穆穆的杜甫

我們是湖
承載著千年中土
的細流。即使
波特萊爾，艾略特
那陣西風和驟雨
不會使我們
湖水變色

我們是山間的湖
也要淙淙地
向歷史流出

We are Lakes

We bear the weight
Of the long flow of time, flowing
Amid the reeds and pebbles
With an articulating Chu Yuan
And a dignified Du Fu

We are lakes
Bearing the weight of the trickle
From the Middle Earth
Over a thousand years. Even the
Western wind or sudden burst of rain
Of Baudelaire of Eliot
Cannot discolor
Our waters

We are mountain lakes
And must ripple
Toward history

Translated by John J.S. Balcom

曾　經

曾經在秋晚強登高樓
風帆點點，卻找不著愁

曾經在紅塵尋一張臉龐
失望是回頭，回頭是失望

在星夜，曾經撐筏渡海
不見林木，但風沙迷漫

也曾經在手術台上徘徊
被壁上的天使輕輕召回

現在，現在已經白髮蕭條
在春水池邊，還學吹簫

Once

I once forced myself to climb a tower one autumn evening
Sails dotted the horizon, but I couldn't find any sorrow

I once sought a face in the dust of this world
Disappointment was looking back, looking back was disappointment

On a starry night, I once rowed across the sea
I saw no forest, but the wind-blown sand was everywhere

I also once wavered on the operating table
Gently called back by the angels on the wall

Now, now my hair is white
At pool's edge in springtime, I still learn to play the flute

Translated by John J.S. Balcom

往　事

當你的烏雲
灑落枕畔的低空
我就騰空躍起
翻覆像一條
出海的龍

當我的鬃毛
在你撫慰的指間
日漸褪色，我只是
一隻跌失前蹄的
千里駒

這些一生的往事
不會載於石刻
卻像一陣
偶然的燕語
落入夕陽的餘暉

Past Events

As your dark hair
Spreads low beside the pillow
I leaped into the air
Rolling like a
Dragon from the sea

As my mane
Gradually whitened beneath
Your comforting fingers, I was a
Winged steed with a
Lame front hoof

These past events from my life
Will not be carved in stone
But like the
Soft chirpings of swallows
Join the afterglow of the setting sun

Translated by John J.S. Balcom

常常想放縱

常常想放縱
在潛意識中
一頭猛獅
或一隻黑狼
在憤怒的時光
總是被我勒住
用一絲自嘲
一句詩、一點宗教

我們都會凶殘若獸
或慈悲如神
僅在俯仰之間
如果你責備我保守
我貼耳俯首

I Always Want to Let Loose

I always want to let loose

In my subconscious

A wild lion

Or a black wolf

In times of wrath

I restrain it

With a modicum of self-mockery

A line of poetry or a bit of religion

We're all capable of ferocity like a beast

Or compassion like a god

In an instant; if you

Reproach my conservatism

I submit

Translated by John J.S. Balcom

鳴　鶴

行年七十還在歌唱
唱自己新譜的曲子
離少年的戀歌日漸遠去
也沒有自悼的意思
每次都當它是最後一闋
人間那得唱幾回

唱得認真，不管別人
驚喜、落淚，或無動於中
永恆若星，或短暫似虹
也任你，聽了隨風拋棄
或在年老的爐邊拾起

我只是一隻掠過世紀的
鳴鶴，短唳長嘯
俯仰間，山河變小

Whooping Crane

At seventy I still have a song to sing

A newly composed song all my own

The love song of youth gradually grows distant

And yet I have no intention of mourning for myself

Each time I consider it the last

Rarely sung more than once in life

Sing for all you're worth, heedless of others

Happy, tearing, or unmoved

Eternal as the stars, fleeting as a rainbow

And it's up to you, to listen and cast aside by the wind

Or gathered by the fireside in old age

I'm just a whooping crane, skimming

Across the centuries, crying briefly or at length

Betwixt movements of the head, the rivers and mountains shrink

Translated by John J.S. Balcom

死亡是如此地沉靜

死亡是如此地沉靜
一塊黑大理石的冰冷
浮雕著欲言又止的雙唇
那氣息倏忽消逝
一匹白馬疾馳而過
名字、只是它的後塵

歡樂和痛苦、愛或恨
未完的戲、或半首詩
此刻都凝成歷史
假如還有未了的韻事
都可以撒手不管
兩手擺一個無奈之姿

青空還在、鳥聲還在
只是不需要再看再聽
花香不遠、恩情未了
從此可以不聞不問
這些都是塵世的騷音
不會再打擾沉睡的眼睛

So Quiet is Death

So quiet is death

The cold of a block of black marble

Carved in relief, lips about to speak

The breath swiftly disappears

A white horse gallops by

Its name, the dust it leaves behind

Happiness and sadness, love and hate

An unfinished play or half a poem

The moment coalesces into history

If there is still an unfinished romantic affair

It can all be laid aside with

A helpless gesture of both hands

The blue sky remains, the chirping of birds too

There's no need to look or listen again

Fragrance of flowers close at hand, grace abounding

Henceforth no interest need be shown

All these disturbing worldly sounds

Can no longer trouble sleeping eyes

Translated by John J.S. Balcom

惘　然

惘然像日落後的天色
氣氳迷漫，從四周合起
也像歷經滄桑的眼色
被水天染得迷離

惘然在沙灘上尋覓
昨日玲瓏的足跡
或看著手堆的雪人
無端端地溶掉眼鼻
惘然，掬起水中的影子
卻從十指間流失
在鬧市中找回記憶
知無結果，依然沉迷

不是痛，不是悲
不是恨，不是懊悔
一封遠年失落的尺素
一陣綿綿的細雨
一串拾不回的春秋
惘然像霧一般昇起
當你回首，坐在搖椅裡

Dejection

My dejection is like the sky after sunset
Wreathed in mist, gathering from all around
It also like the look that shows life's vicissitudes
Blurred by water and sky

Dejected, I walk the beach seeking
Yesterday's exquisite footprints
Or watch as the features of a snowman
Melt away for no apparent reason
Dejected, I scoop my reflection out of the water
Only to have it flow away between my fingers
Or, in the bustling city, I call up memories
Knowing there'll be no outcome, still I indulge

Neither pain nor sadness
Neither hate nor regret
A long lost letter
A long drizzle
An irrecoverable age
My dejection rises like the fog
As you look back, sitting in a rocking chair

Translated by John J.S. Balcom

對流

CONVECTION

譯者簡介 Translator
余光中（Yu Kwang-chung）

余光中，1928年生。現為位於台灣高雄的國立中山大學榮譽教授。一位創作等身和多才多藝的作家，曾在台灣、香港及大陸出版八十餘本詩、散文、評論及翻譯作品；也曾在台港得過無數大獎包括1991年香港翻譯學會的殊榮：榮譽會員Honorary Fellowship。從1990到1998余氏曾任台北中華筆會的會長。

Born in 1928, Yu Kwang-chung is now Honored Professor at National Sun Yat-sen University in Kaohsiung, Taiwan. A prolific and versatile writer, he has published in Taiwan, Hong Kong and mainland China more than eighty books, most of which are verses and the rest are prose, criticism, and translations. Recipient of a dozen major literary awards in Taiwan and Hong Kong, he was conferred an honorary fellowship by the Hong Kong Translation Society in 1991. From 1990 to 1998 he was President of the Taipei Chinese PEN Center.

雨　中

只為了遠遠的一絲光，
一閃笑靨，一顆願望，
或久藏在心窖裏的一罈
友情。我們奔走在雨中。
讓脊髓如蛇般冰涼，
（額骨落下了簷滴）
讓雨景掛在別人的牆上。

在雨中，我們內裏的爐火
瀕臨熄滅，體溫的水銀柱
在渴望某種心靈的燃料。
在雨中，煩惱降下了
無數青絲，憂鬱昇起
遠山的面幕。
雖然，我們知道
這些都是暫時的。

那些為了溫暖的片刻
捱受整冬的風雪，
為了看一顆無名星

In the Rain

Just for a trace of light far away,

A flash of smile, a bud of hope,

Or a cask of friendship cellared long

In the heart, we walk in the rain

And let our spines snake-like freeze,

(While water drips down the eaves of our brows)

And let the rainy scene hang on others' walls.

In the rain the fire in us often threatens

To die out, the mercury of our bodily warmth

Yearns for certain psychic fuels.

In the rain there falls a net

Of gossamers of fret, and sorrow draws

A veil over the distant hills.

Yet we know

These come and go.

Those who for a moment of warmth

Brave the snowstorms of a whole winter,

And for a glimpse of a nameless star

失足在斷崖的人，
值得我們尊敬。

那些想在雨中跳恰恰
怕沾污了羽毛；
想展覽思想的傑作
怕缺少知音；
欲炫耀金幣
又怕發綠的人，
值得我們憐憫。

在這世紀的風雨中，
等待陽光原是一種虐待；
飲清醒的歲月，更需自制。
我們不禁要問：
「這暫時的風雨，
會籠罩我們忍受的一生？」

在雨中，我們詛咒左腳，
安慰右腳。俯視現實的泥沼，
仰望空中的幻景。
雖然，我們知道：
這些都是暫時的──
就像那虹。

Stumble over a precipice,
Are worthy of our respect.

Those who want to dance in the rain,
Yet are afraid to soil their plumes,
Who want to display their minds' works,
Yet fear a lack of audience,
Who want to show off their gold coins,
Yet are afraid they'll turn green with mildew,
Our pity well deserve.

In the storm of the century
It's an ordeal to wait for the sun.
To drink the soberness of the years
Requires self-restraint of us.
We cannot help asking:
"Will the tempestuous moment last
The tortured length of our lives?"

In the rain we curse the left foot
And bless the right. Into reality's puddles
We look, and gaze up at mirages in the sky.
Yet we know
These come and go —
As does the rainbow.

Translated by Yu Kwang-chung

士大夫

我們尚活在晉代，
留著長長的指甲。

欲哭窮途，
沒有阮籍的眼淚，
不想折腰
歸無淵明的田園。

還是坐在竹林下
清談清談罷！
從德先生到賽先生，
從賽先生到德先生。

The Literati

We still live in the Chin Dynasty[1]
And keep our fingernails long.

We want to weep at the road's end,
But cannot shed Juan Chi's tears;[2]
We abhor bowing to bureaucrats,
But cannot go home to T'ao Ch'ien's farm.[3]

Might as well sit in a bamboo grove
And have a transcendental talk
From Mr. Teh to Mr. Sai,
From Mr. Sai to Mr. Teh.[4]

這樣，我們就晉入了
開元之治？

註：與其空談泛泛，不若從日常瑣事中著手改革，身體力行，或可挽回社
　　會風氣於一日。此係作者對中西文化問題之一種看法。

Shall we thus enter

The golden age of K'ai-yuan?[5]

Translated by Yu Kwang-chung

[1] Chin Dynasty (265-420) was a period in Chinese history when Taoism prevailed and the elite spent more time in idle and brilliant conversation than in immediate action. It is thus associated with intellectual escapism.

[2] Juan Chi (210-263) was an eccentric scholar-poet who would trace a road up a hill and, coming to its end, weep, bitterly before he turned back.

[3] T'ao Ch'ien (327-427), the greatest poet between Ch'u Yuan and the T'ang masters, resigned his office as Magistrate of P'eng-tse because, as he said, he hated to bow to senior officials for a dole of five pecks of rice.

[4] Teh and Sai are playful approximations in Chinese pronunciation for the initial sounds of "democracy" and "science," two aspects of Western civilization advocated by Dr. Hu Shih and other leaders of the May Fourth Movement.

[5] K'ai-yuan (713-742) was the title of the early reign of Emperor Hsuan-tsung of the T'ang Dynasty, one of the most prestigious periods in Chinese history.

自由神像

好風從八方吹來，
自由神的裙裾飄拂著。
那些船——
　　小得像玩具，
　　出沒若幽靈。
來自驚慌的歐羅巴，
騷動的非洲，
和多難的亞細亞。

進港的人，
誰能看見她掙斷的腳鐐？
只見她手中的火炬。
（擎得更高呀！
這世界還是很暗，很冷。）

她是法蘭西的千金，
美利堅的女神，
千千萬萬尋求自由的
　　夢中的情人。

Statue of Liberty

In the fair winds from all quarters
The Goddess of Liberty's skirt flows.
All those ships —
　　Tiny as toys,
　　Haunting as ghosts,
From alarms of Europe are come,
From agitations of Africa,
From disasters of Asia.

Of all the people entering the harbor
Who sees the shackles she broke loose?
They only see the torch in her hand.
(Hold it higher, higher!
The world is still so dark, so cold.)

She is the Daughter of France,
The Goddess of America,
The dream lover
　　of thousands longing to be free.

遠遠從海上望去，
她是一尊維納斯的誕生。

然而，她熟悉周圍的風景——
聯合國遠得像一塊
　　未曾銘刻的白碑；
勃洛克林橋是一隻
　　人類久廢的豎琴；
而曼哈頓區只是
　　二十世紀的蜃樓海市。

好風從八方吹來，
她卻在諦聽
背後西伯利亞的寒流，
卻在守望，起自
中南美洲的Hurricane。

註：此詩寫于1963年。

Seen at a distance on the sea,
She is Venus just given birth.

Yet she is at home with the scene around —
The UN Building remote as
    A white tombstone yet uncarved;
The Brooklyn Bridge is a harp
    Long unused by mankind;
Manhattan Island is only
    A twentieth-century mirage.

In the fair winds from all quarters
Intently does she listen
To the cold Siberian blast at her back
And watch out on hurricanes
From Central and South Americas.

Note: This poem was written in 1963.

Translated by Yu Kwang-chung

對流

CONVECTION

譯者簡介 Translator
馬嵬（Wei Ma）

　　馬嵬，1957生於蘇州。蘇州大學外語系畢業，上海復旦大學文學碩士。曾任蘇州大學副教授，專研古典英詩。來美後，又獲紐約大學工商管理碩士（MBA）。現任紐約一個著名律師事務所的資訊技術部門主管。

　　Wei Ma was born in 1957, a native of Suzhou, China. He holds a B.A. degree from Suzhou University and an M.A. degree from Fudan University, Shanghai, both in English literature. Before he came to America, he was teaching at Suzhou University. His interest is in classic English poetry. With an MBA from the City University of New York, he now holds the position of Director of Information Technology at a large law firm in New York City.

樹

樹，你是我唯一的知心，
當我在寂寞，無告，黯然之境。

你那輕輕慰藉的語氣，
使我把世俗的愛恨，一齊拋棄。

你那舉手擺腰的舞姿，
使我將童年的歡愉，重溫一次。

你那裸足散髮的神態，
使我對大自然的樸真，格外熱愛。

不止一次，我陶醉於你的髮香，
當你浴罷，將它梳理得清爽發亮。

不止一次，你哼著抒情的小調，
當我獨靠在你腳邊，出神遠眺。

樹啊！有一天我將和你合而為一，
那時，我躺在你足下，無聲無息。

Trees

O trees! The best companion of my soul
When in solitude unspoken I stroll.

For your whisper is so sweet and tender
That worldly love and hate I'd surrender.

The pose of your hands a twist of your waist
So charming, pleasure of childhood again I taste.

Your bare feet and your windblown hair
Are Nature's simple beauty I so deeply care.

Oft, I adored your bright and fragrant hair,
Fresh after shower, tidied smooth and fair.

Oft, I leaned against your trunk allowing
Fancies to roam with your lovely humming.

O trees! Some day you and I will unite
When under your feet in silence I reside.

Translated by Wei Ma

給凱蒂

我不敢親一親你的小嘴，
太紅太熱，使人昏醉。
啊！凱蒂！
我只想偷吻妳的髮際，
那裏有草葉清香的氣息！

我願化成隻神秘的蝴蝶，
白天歇在妳柔軟的草地，
啊！凱蒂！
等到妳失眠的夜晚來臨，
用我夢幻的翅膀將塵世隔離！

To Katie

I dare not kiss your small lips,

So red, so warm, as to cast a spell.

O Katie!

May I but steal a kiss on your hair tips,

The fresh and fragrant grass to smell!

I wish I were a mystic butterfly

That rests on your soft grass for the day;

O Katie!

When sleepless in night you lie

My wings will screen the noisy world away!

Translated by Wei Ma

閉目，死

倦鷹的收翅，幕之落；
最後的螢光，在眼中
若隕星般一閃爍。

水閘已放下，溪流漸停；
大海將封凍，不再起伏。
腦的天際充滿了沉沉鉛雲。

生命的太陽已沒入地平線，
黑暗來襲，窗已失明，
一幅莊嚴的暮色在臉上完成。

肉體的園門戛然而閉──
一如往昔神秘的開；
靈魂那流浪者從此無依。

一則故事，一幕劇，一段歷史
已完成。擱筆，止。

Eyes Closed, Dead

Folded wings of a soaring hawk,
Drawn curtains on the stage,
The last glow in the eyes
Flashes like a falling star in the sky.

The gate's been lowered, the stream coming to a halt;
Oceans are freezing, waves no longer moving ahead;
The firmament of spirit is loaded with clouds of lead.

The sun in the horizon has declined.
Darkness is now rampant, and windows become blind:
The grand dusk on the face is finally completed.

Passage to the body is shut in a sudden —
Just as in mystery it was first open;
The tramping soul is once again on the road.

A story, a play, a history
Is finished. The pen is dropped. FIN.

Translated by Wei Ma

胡適，未完成的塑像

雕塑家楊英風工作室中有胡適之先生未完成塑像一尊，
略具眉目，覆以塑膠布。旁掛胡先生遺像一幀，笑容可
掬，像在要說些什麼。

如此容易觸及，如此遠，
如此可以辨認，又如此模糊；
隔著一層半透明的覆蓋，
若死亡之面幕。

你的容貌猶未完成，
如在三月的母胎。
你的丰采、你的聲音，
尚在泥土之中
待著春天，待著捏塑。

那平凡的泥土
將化為你的肉身，
當你偉大的肉身
正還原成泥土。

Hu Shih, an Unfinished Sculpture[*]

So close to reach, yet so far away,

So easy to see, yet so dull in clay;

A half-transparent sheet covers your head

Like a white mask over someone dead.

Your features still need the final touch,

Like a growing fetus in the third month pregnancy;

Your voice, and your elegancy

Remain buried in the clay as such

Waiting for the coming of Spring, for the crafty hand.

The plain and earthy clay

Will soon become your body,

While your glorious body

Does now to clay restore.

而壁上的那幀
如一個神秘的證人；
笑對這座塑像，
觀照一次重生。

在你寬大的袍內
有五千年的胸襟；
在你著名的笑容後
有一條不移的定律。
你的眼神，悲憫著
這寒氣未消的二月。
你的雙耳在傾聽
古老的中國榆樹上
啄木鳥的叩聲。

唉！從死亡裏
你留下的果子，
被我們不經心地失落了！
現在，霧還是霧，
咳嗽的人，還在咳嗽。
那些哀悼過你的
坐下來替別人寫讚辭；
那些送殯的青年，
已去海外雲遊。

The portrait on the wall is all this while

Looking like a mystic witness

At the sculpture with a gentle smile,

Contemplating himself coming to life again.

Your large robe, home to your liberal soul,

Accommodates a history five thousand years old.

Your smile, so typical of you,

Conveys a law that is forever true.

You look on with deep compassion

In this still chilly February;

You listen with all attention

To the woodpecker's knocking

On an old Chinese elm tree.

Alas! Where is your legacy?

The seeds you left us

But have been lost carelessly by us?

Now, the fog is still the fog,

The people who coughed are still coughing,

Those who mourned your death

Are writing to glorify somebody else,

And the youths to your funeral who came

Have gone on a tour abroad all the same.

如一輪霧中之日，
你需要重新誕生
在這個古國，在這塊荒原。
當歷史的竹簡執於顫顫
的手中。當年輕的血液
流向苟安的時辰。

你已向歷史
塑成了永恆的微笑，
春來時
它將是迎面的蒲公英。

對你的塑像──
尚待我們自心底完成。

一九六三年二月二十二日寫於
胡適之先生逝世一週年前夕

Like the sun in the mist,

On a new life you need to insist.

In this ancient country, this wasteland,

When History's bamboo-slips are in a shaky hand,

And the young blood rushes

Toward a moment of temporary peace.

To History you have already carved yourself

Into an eternal smile,

Which shall become greeting dandelions everywhere

When Spring is in the air.

The making of your sculpture —

Shall be finished inside everyone's heart.

Translated by Wei Ma

* Hu Shih（胡適）, 1891-1962, great educator and philosopher of modern day China. This poem was written in 1963 when a sculpture of his was still under making by a famous artist, Yu-yu Yang（楊英風）。

CONVECTION

閱讀大詩26　PG1135

 對流
　　——夏菁中英對照詩集

編　　著	夏　菁
責任編輯	劉　璞
圖文排版	詹凱倫
封面設計	陳怡捷

出版策劃	釀出版
製作發行	秀威資訊科技股份有限公司
	114 台北市內湖區瑞光路76巷65號1樓
	電話：+886-2-2796-3638　傳真：+886-2-2796-1377
	服務信箱：service@showwe.com.tw
	http://www.showwe.com.tw
郵政劃撥	19563868　戶名：秀威資訊科技股份有限公司
展售門市	國家書店【松江門市】
	104 台北市中山區松江路209號1樓
	電話：+886-2-2518-0207　傳真：+886-2-2518-0778
網路訂購	秀威網路書店：http://www.bodbooks.com.tw
	國家網路書店：http://www.govbooks.com.tw
法律顧問	毛國樑　律師
總 經 銷	聯合發行股份有限公司
	地址：231新北市新店區寶橋路235巷6弄6號4樓
	電話：+886-2-2917-8022　傳真：+886-2-2915-6275

出版日期	2014年3月　BOD一版
定　　價	270元

國家圖書館出版品預行編目

對流 : 夏菁中英對照詩集 / 夏菁編著. -- 一版. -- 臺北
市 : 釀出版, 2014.03
　　面 ；　公分. -- (閱讀大詩 ; 26)
　BOD版
　ISBN 978-986-5871-99-4 (平裝)

813.1　　　　　　　　　　　　　　　　103001712

讀 者 回 函 卡

感謝您購買本書，為提升服務品質，請填妥以下資料，將讀者回函卡直接寄回或傳真本公司，收到您的寶貴意見後，我們會收藏記錄及檢討，謝謝！

如您需要了解本公司最新出版書目、購書優惠或企劃活動，歡迎您上網查詢或下載相關資料：http:// www.showwe.com.tw

您購買的書名：_____

出生日期：_____年_____月_____日

學歷：□高中 (含) 以下　　□大專　　□研究所 (含) 以上

職業：□製造業　□金融業　□資訊業　□軍警　□傳播業　□自由業

　　　□服務業　□公務員　□教職　□學生　□家管　□其它_____

購書地點：□網路書店　□實體書店　□書展　□郵購　□贈閱　□其他

您從何得知本書的消息？

　□網路書店　□實體書店　□網路搜尋　□電子報　□書訊　□雜誌

　□傳播媒體　□親友推薦　□網站推薦　□部落格　□其他_____

您對本書的評價：（請填代號　1.非常滿意　2.滿意　3.尚可　4.再改進）

　封面設計____　版面編排____　內容____　文／譯筆____　價格____

讀完書後您覺得：

　□很有收穫　□有收穫　□收穫不多　□沒收穫

對我們的建議：_____

_____

_____

_____

11466
台北市內湖區瑞光路 76 巷 65 號 1 樓

秀威資訊科技股份有限公司　　　收

BOD 數位出版事業部

....

（請沿線對折寄回，謝謝！）

姓　　名：＿＿＿＿＿＿＿＿　年齡：＿＿＿＿　性別：□女　□男

郵遞區號：□□□□□

地　　址：＿＿＿＿＿＿＿＿＿＿＿＿＿＿＿＿＿＿＿＿＿

聯絡電話：(日)＿＿＿＿＿＿＿＿　(夜)＿＿＿＿＿＿＿＿＿

E-mail：＿＿＿＿＿＿＿＿＿＿＿＿＿＿＿＿＿＿＿＿＿